FOR ANTOINETTE

Library of Congress Cataloging-in-Publication Data:

Watkins, Rowboat, 1967- author.
Rude cakes / cooked up by Rowboat Watkins. — 1st edition.
pages cm
Summary: A story about rude cake who never says please or thank you or listens to its parents, and a Giant
Cyclops who is polite.
ISBN 978-1-4521-3851-0 (alk. paper)
1. Courtesy—Juvenile fiction. 2. Conduct of life—Juvenile fiction. 3. Cake—Juvenile fiction. [1. Etiquette—
Fiction.. 2. Conduct of life—Fiction. 3. Cake—Fiction.] I. Title.

PZ7.1.W4Ru 2015
[E]—dc23

2014026316

Manufactured in China.

Design by Rowboat Watkins and Sara Gillingham Studio.
The pictures in this book were made with a pinch of pencil,
a dash of ink, and baked in an iMac.

10 9 8 7 6 5 4 3 2

Chronicle Books LLC
680 Second Street
San Francisco, California 94107

Chronicle Books—we see things differently.
Become part of our community at www.chroniclekids.com.

RUDE CAKES

COOKED UP BY Rowboat Watkins

chronicle books · san francisco

HURRY!

Rude cakes never say please,

and they never say
thank you,

and they sometimes take things

that don't belong to them.

Rude cakes never listen

(especially when their parents sound boring)

and they never

BACK OFF!

wait their turn in line.

Rude cakes never share,

and they're never sorry

because they're never, ever wrong.

They also think baths are dumb

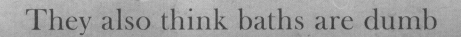

SERIOUSLY...
I'M A CAKE...
HOW DIRTY
CAN I BE?

and that bedtime is for donut holes.

Oddly enough . . .

GIANT
CYCLOPSES

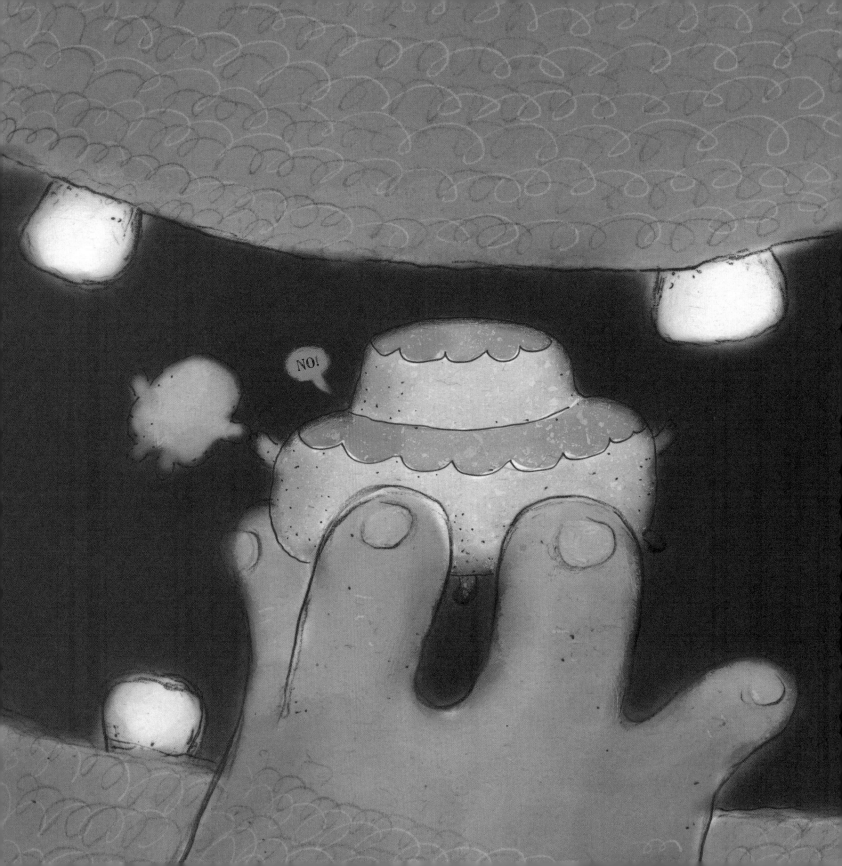

to wear jaunty little hats.

Giant Cyclopses always say thank you,

and they always say please,

and they love to share.

Giant Cyclopses also LOVE
to wait their turn in line.

Giant Cyclopses always listen when
their hats say please, nicely

(even if what they hear sounds boring)

and they always apologize when they're wrong.

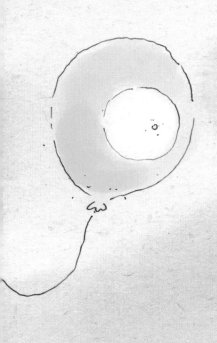
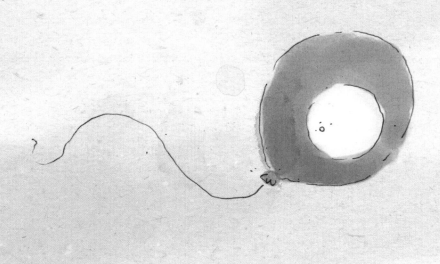

Of course, no cake
is ever too rude
to change.

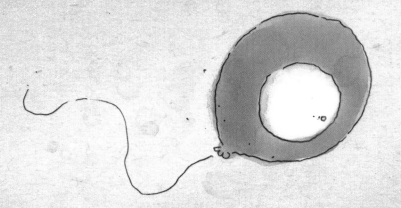